PENGUIN CLASSICS

GOD'S TROMBONES

JAMES WELDON JOHNSON was born in Jacksonville, Florida, in 1871. Among the first to break through the barriers segregating his race, he was educated at Atlanta University and at Columbia, and was the first black admitted to the Florida bar. He was also, for a time, a songwriter in New York, American consul in Venezuela and Nicaragua, executive secretary of the NAACP, and professor of creative literature at Fisk University—experiences recorded in his autobiography, *Along This Way*. Other books by him include *Saint Peter Relates an Incident, Black Manhattan*, and *God's Trombones: Seven Negro Sermons in Verse*. In addition to his own writing, Johnson was the editor of pioneering anthologies of black American poetry and spirituals. He died in 1938.

MAYA ANGELOU is a celebrated poet, educator, historian, best-selling author, actress, playwright, civil rights activist, producer, and director. She is the author of twelve best-selling books, including *I Know Why the Caged Bird Sings* (1970) and *A Song Flung Up to Heaven* (2002). In 1981, Dr. Angelou was appointed to a lifetime position as the first Reynolds Professor of American Studies at Wake Forest University. In January 1993, she became only the second poet in U.S. history to have the honor of writing and reciting original work at the presidential inauguration.

HENRY LOUIS GATES, JR., is Alphonse Fletcher University Professor and director of the W. E. B. Du Bois Institute for African and African American Research at Harvard University. He is editor in chief of the Oxford African American Studies Center. His most recent books are *America Behind the Color Line: Dialogues with African Americans* (Warner Books, 2004), *African American Lives*, coedited with Evelyn Brooks Higginbotham (Oxford, 2004), and *The Annotated Uncle Tom's Cabin*, edited with Hollis Robbins (W. W. Norton, 2006). *Finding Oprah's Roots*, his latest book and documentary project, a meditation on genetics, genealogy, and race, was published by Crown in February 2007. In 2006,

Professor Gates wrote and produced the PBS documentary also called *African American Lives*. He also wrote and produced the documentaries *Wonders of the African World* (2000) and *America Beyond the Color Line* (2004) for the BBC and PBS, and authored the companion volumes to both series. A four-hour sequel to *African American Lives* aired in February 2008.

JAMES WELDON JOHNSON

God's Trombones
Seven Negro Sermons in Verse

Foreword by MAYA ANGELOU
General Editor: HENRY LOUIS GATES, JR.

PENGUIN BOOKS

PENGUIN BOOKS
Published by the Penguin Group
Penguin Group (USA) Inc., 375 Hudson Street, New York, New York 10014, U.S.A.
Penguin Group (Canada), 90 Eglinton Avenue East, Suite 700, Toronto,
Ontario, Canada M4P 2Y3 (a division of Pearson Penguin Canada Inc.)
Penguin Books Ltd, 80 Strand, London WC2R 0RL, England
Penguin Ireland, 25 St Stephen's Green, Dublin 2, Ireland (a division of Penguin Books Ltd)
Penguin Group (Australia), 250 Camberwell Road, Camberwell,
Victoria, 3124, Australia (a division of Pearson Australia Group Pty Ltd)
Penguin Books India Pvt Ltd, 11 Community Centre,
Panchsheel Park, New Delhi–110 017, India
Penguin Group (NZ), 67 Apollo Drive, Rosedale, North Shore 0632,
New Zealand (a division of Pearson New Zealand Ltd)
Penguin Books (South Africa) (Pty) Ltd, 24 Sturdee Avenue,
Rosebank, Johannesburg 2196, South Africa

Penguin Books Ltd, Registered Offices:
80 Strand, London WC2R 0RL, England

First published in the United States of America by the Viking Press, Inc. 1927
Published in a Viking Compass edition 1969
Published in Penguin Books 1976
This edition with a foreword by Maya Angelou and
an introduction by Henry Louis Gates, Jr., published 2008

1 3 5 7 9 10 8 6 4 2

Copyright The Viking Press, Inc., 1927
Copyright renewed Grace Nail Johnson, 1955
Foreword copyright © Maya Angelou, 2008
Introduction copyright © Henry Louis Gates, Jr., 2008
All rights reserved

LIBRARY OF CONGRESS CATALOGING IN PUBLICATION DATA
Johnson, James Weldon, 1871–1938.
God's trombones : seven Negro sermons in verse / James Weldon Johnson ; foreword by
Maya Angelou ; general editor Henry Louis Gates, Jr.—[Rev. ed.]
p.   cm.—(Penguin classics)
ISBN 978-0-14-310541-1 (hc.)
ISBN 978-0-14-310541-1 (pbk.)
I. Gates, Henry Louis. II. Title.
PS3519.O2625G6 2008
811'.52—dc22   2008008886

Printed in the United States of America
Set in Sabon

To Arthur B. Spingarn

Contents

Acknowledgments

Grateful acknowledgment is made for the kind permission to reprint the following poems: to *The Freeman* for "The Creation," to *The American Mercury* for "Go Down Death," and to *The Century Magazine* for "The Judgment Day."

What Is an African American Classic?

I have long nurtured a deep and abiding affection for the Penguin Classics, at least since I was an undergraduate at Yale. I used to imagine that my attraction for these books—grouped together, as a set, in some independent bookstores when I was a student, and perhaps even in some today—stemmed from the fact that my first-grade classmates, for some reason that I can't recall, were required to dress as penguins in our annual all-school pageant, and perform a collective side-to side motion that our misguided teacher thought she could choreograph into something meant to pass for a "dance." Piedmont, West Virginia, in 1956, was a very long way from Penguin Nation, wherever that was supposed to be! But penguins we were determined to be, and we did our level best to avoid wounding each other with our orange-colored cardboard beaks while stomping out of rhythm in our matching orange, veined webbed feet. The whole scene was madness, one never to be repeated at the Davis Free School. But I never stopped loving penguins. And I have never stopped loving the very audacity of the idea of the Penguin Classics, an affordable, accessible library of the most important and compelling texts in the history of civilization, their black-and-white spines and covers and uniform type giving each text a comfortable, familiar feel, as if we have encountered it, or its cousins, before. I think of the Penguin Classics as the very best and most compelling in human thought, an Alexandrian library in paperback, enclosed in black and white.

I still gravitate to the Penguin Classics when killing time in an airport bookstore, deferring the slow torture of the security lines. Sometimes I even purchase two or three, fantasizing that I can speed-read one of the shorter titles, then make a dent in the longer one, vainly attempting to fill the holes in the liberal arts education that our degrees suggest we have, over the course of a plane ride! Mark Twain once quipped that a classic is "something that everybody wants to have read and nobody wants to read," and perhaps that applies to my airport purchasing habits. For my generation, these titles in the Penguin Classics form the canon—the canon of the texts that a truly well-educated person should have read, and read carefully and closely, at least once. For years I rued the absence of texts by black authors in this series, and longed to be able to make even a small contribution to the diversification of this astonishingly universal list. I watched with great pleasure as titles by African American and African authors began to appear, some two dozen over the past several years. So when Elda Rotor approached me about editing a series of African American classics and collections for Penguin's Portable Series, I eagerly accepted.

Thinking about the titles appropriate for inclusion in this series led me, inevitably, to think about what, for me, constitutes a "classic." And thinking about this led me, in turn, to the wealth of reflections on what defines a work of literature or philosophy somehow speaking to the human condition beyond time and place, a work somehow endlessly compelling, generation upon generation, a work whose author we don't have to look like to identify with, to feel at one with, as we find ourselves transported through the magic of a textual time machine; a work that refracts the image of ourselves that we project onto it, regardless of our ethnicity, our gender, our time, our place. This is what centuries of scholars and writers have meant when they use the word "classic," and—despite all that we know about the complex intersubjectivity of the production of meaning in the wondrous exchange between a reader and a text—it remains true that classic texts, even in the most conventional, conservative sense of the word "classic," do exist, and these books will continue to be read long after the generation the text reflects and defines, the generation of readers contemporary with the text's author, is dead and gone. Classic texts speak from their authors' graves, in their names, in their voices. As Italo Calvino once remarked, "A classic is a book that has never finished saying what it has to say."

Faulkner put this idea in an interesting way: "The aim of every artist is to arrest motion, which is life, by artificial means, and hold it fixed so that a hundred years later, when a stranger looks at it, it moves again since it is life." That, I am certain, must be the desire of every writer. But what about the reader? What makes a book a classic to a reader? Here, perhaps, Hemingway said it best: "All good books are alike in that they are truer than if they had really happened and after you are finished reading one you will feel that all that happened to you, and afterwards it belongs to you, the good and the bad, the ecstasy, the remorse and sorrow, the people and the places and how the weather was."

I have been reading black literature since I was fifteen, yanked into that dark discursive universe by an Episcopal priest at a church camp near my home in West Virginia in August of 1965, during the terrifying days of the Watts Riots in Los Angeles. Eventually, by fits and starts, studying the literature written by black authors became my avocation; ultimately, it has become my vocation. And, in my own way, I have tried to be an evangelist for it, to a readership larger than my own people, people who, as it were, look like these texts. Here, I am reminded of something W. S. Merwin said about the books he most loved: "Perhaps a classic is a work that one imagines should be common knowledge, but more and more often isn't." I would say, of African and African American literature, that perhaps classic works by black writers are works that one imagines should be common knowledge among the broadest possible readership but that less and less are, as the teaching of reading to understand how words can create the worlds into which books can transport us yields to classroom instruction geared toward passing a state-authorized, standardized exam. All literary texts suffer from this wrongheaded approach to teaching, mind you; but it especially affects texts by people of

color, and texts by women—texts still struggling, despite enor-
mous gains over the last twenty years, to gain a solid foothold
in anthologies and syllabi. For every anthology, every syllabus,
every publishing series such as the Penguin Classics constitutes
a distinct "canon," an implicit definition of all that is essential
for a truly educated person to read.

James Baldwin, who has pride of place in my personal canon
of African American authors since it was one of his books that
that Episcopal priest gave me to read in that dreadful summer
of 1965, argued that "the responsibility of a writer is to exca-
vate the experience of the people who produced him." But surely
Baldwin would have agreed with E. M. Forster that the books
that we remember, the books that have truly influenced us, are
those that "have gone a little further down our particular path
than we have yet ourselves." Excavating the known is a worthy
goal of the writer as cultural archaeologist; yet, at the same
time, so is unveiling the unknown, the unarticulated yet shared
experience of the colorless things that make us human: "some-
thing we have always known (or thought we knew)," as Calvino
puts it, "but without knowing that this author said it first." We
might think of the difference between Forster and Baldwin,
on the one hand, and Calvino, on the other, as the difference
between an author representing what has happened (Forster,
Baldwin) in the history of a people whose stories, whose very
history itself, has long been suppressed, and what could have
happened (Calvino) in the atemporal realm of art. This is an
important distinction when thinking about the nature of an
African American classic—rather, when thinking about the
nature of the texts that comprise the African American liter-
ary tradition, or, for that matter, the texts in any underread
tradition.

One of James Baldwin's most memorable essays, a subtle
meditation on sexual preference, race, and gender, is entitled
"Here Be Dragons." So much of traditional African American
literature, even fiction and poetry—ostensibly at least once re-
moved from direct statement—was meant to deal a fatal blow
to the dragon of racism. For black writers since the eighteenth-
century beginnings of the tradition, literature has been one

more weapon—a very important weapon, mind you, but still one weapon among many—in the arsenal black people have drawn upon to fight against antiblack racism and for their equal rights before the law. Ted Joans, the black surrealist poet, called this sort of literature from the sixties' Black Arts movement "hand grenade poems"! Of what possible use are the niceties of figuration when one must slay a dragon? I can hear you say give me the blunt weapon anytime! Problem is, it is more difficult than some writers seem to think to slay a dragon with a poem or a novel. Social problems persist; literature too tied to addressing those social problems tends to enter the historical archives, leaving the realm of the literary. Let me state bluntly what should be obvious: writers are read for how they write, not what they write about.

Frederick Douglass—for this generation of readers one of the most widely read statesman-reformer-writers—reflected on this matter even in the midst of one of his most fiery speeches addressing the ironies of the sons and daughters of slaves celebrating the Fourth of July while slavery continued unabated. In his now-classic essay "What to the Slave Is the Fourth of July?" (1852), Douglass argued that an immediate, almost transparent form of discourse was demanded of black writers by the heated temper of the times, a discourse with an immediate end in mind: "At a time like this, scorching irony, not convincing argument, is needed. . . . a fiery stream of biting ridicule, blasting reproach, withering sarcasm, and stern rebuke. For it is not light that is needed, but fire, it is not a gentle shower, but thunder. We need the storm, the whirlwind, and earthquake." Above all else, Douglass concludes, the rhetoric of the literature created by African Americans must, of necessity, be a purposeful rhetoric, its ends targeted at attacking the evils that afflict black people: "The feeling of the nation must be quickened; the conscience of the nation must be roused; the propriety of the nation must be startled; the hypocrisy of the nation must be exposed; and its crimes against God and man must be proclaimed and denounced." And perhaps this was so; nevertheless, we read Douglass's writings today in literature classes not so much for their content but to understand, and marvel at,

his sublime mastery of words, words—to paraphrase Calvino—
that never finish saying what it is they have to say, not because
of their "message," but because of the language in which that
message is inextricably enfolded.

There are as many ways to define a classic in the African
American tradition as there are in any other tradition, and
these ways are legion. So many essays have been published en-
titled "What Is a Classic?" that they could fill several large an-
thologies. And while no one can say explicitly why generations
of readers return to read certain texts, just about everyone can
agree that making a best-seller list in one's lifetime is most cer-
tainly not an index of fame or influence over time; the longevity
of one's readership—of books about which one says "I am
rereading," as Calvino puts it—on the other hand, most cer-
tainly is. So, the size of one's readership (through library use,
Internet access, and sales) cumulatively is an interesting factor
to consider; and because of series such as the Penguin Classics,
we can gain a sense, for our purposes, of those texts written by
authors in previous generations that have sustained sales—
mostly for classroom use—long after their authors were dead.

There can be little doubt that *The Narrative of the Life of
Frederick Douglass* (1845), *The Souls of Black Folk* (1903), by
W. E. B. Du Bois, and *Their Eyes Were Watching God* (1937),
by Zora Neale Hurston, are the three most classic of the black
classics—again, as measured by consumption—while Langston
Hughes's poetry, though not purchased as books in these large
numbers, is accessed through the Internet as frequently as that
of any other American poet, and indeed profoundly more so
than most. Within Penguin's Portable Series list, the most pop-
ular individual titles, excluding Douglass's first slave narrative
and Du Bois's *Souls,* are:

Up from Slavery (1903), Booker T. Washington
The Autobiography of an Ex-Coloured Man (1912), James
    Weldon Johnson
God's Trombones (1927), James Weldon Johnson
Passing (1929), Nella Larsen
The Marrow of Tradition (1898), Charles W. Chesnutt

Incidents in the Life of a Slave Girl (1861), Harriet Jacobs
The Interesting Narrative (1789), Olaudah Equiano
The House Behind the Cedars (1900), Charles W. Chesnutt
My Bondage and My Freedom (1855), Frederick Douglass
Quicksand (1928), Nella Larsen

These titles form a canon of classics of African American literature, judged by classroom readership. If we add Jean Toomer's novel *Cane* (1922), arguably the first work of African American modernism, along with Douglass's first narrative, Du Bois's *The Souls,* and Hurston's *Their Eyes,* we would most certainly have included many of the touchstones of black literature published before 1940, when Richard Wright published *Native Son.*

Every teacher's syllabus constitutes a canon of sorts, and I teach these texts and a few others as the classics of the black canon. Why these particular texts? I can think of two reasons: First, these texts signify or riff upon each other, repeating, borrowing, and extending metaphors book to book, generation to generation. To take just a few examples, Equiano's eighteenth-century use of the trope of the talking book (an image found, remarkably, in five slave narratives published between 1770 and 1811) becomes, with Frederick Douglass, the representation of the quest for freedom as, necessarily, the quest for literacy, for a freedom larger than physical manumission; we might think of this as the representation of metaphysical manumission, of freedom and literacy—the literacy of great literature—inextricably intertwined. Douglass transformed the metaphor of the talking book into the trope of chiasmus, a repetition with a stinging reversal: "You have seen how a man becomes a slave, you will see how a slave becomes a man." Du Bois, with Douglass very much on his mind, transmuted chiasmus a half century later into the metaphor of duality or double consciousness, a necessary condition of living one's life, as he memorably put it, behind a "veil."

Du Bois's metaphor has a powerful legacy in twentieth-century black fiction: James Weldon Johnson, in *The Ex-Coloured Man,* literalizes the trope of double consciousness by depicting as his protagonist a man who, at will, can occupy two distinct racial spaces, one black, one white, and who moves seamlessly, if ruefully, between them; Toomer's *Cane* takes Du Bois's metaphor of duality for the inevitably split consciousness that every Negro must feel living in a country in which her or his status as a citizen is liminal at best, or has been erased at worst, and makes of this the metaphor for the human condition itself under modernity, a tellingly bold rhetorical gesture—one designed to make the Negro the metaphor of the human condition. And Hurston, in *Their Eyes,* extends Toomer's revision even further, depicting a character who can only gain her voice once she can name this condition of duality or double consciousness and then glide gracefully and lyrically between her two selves, an "inside" self and an "outside" one.

More recently, Alice Walker, in *The Color Purple,* signifies upon two aspects of the narrative strategy of *Their Eyes*: first, she revisits the theme of a young black woman finding her voice, depicting a protagonist who writes herself into being through letters addressed to God and to her sister, Nettie— letters that grow ever more sophisticated in their syntax and grammar and imagery as she comes to consciousness before our very eyes, letter to letter; and second, Walker riffs on Hurston's use of a vernacular-inflected free indirect discourse to show that black English has the capacity to serve as the medium for narrating a novel through the black dialect that forms a most pliable and expansive language in Celie's letters. Ralph Ellison makes Du Bois's metaphor of the veil a trope of blindness and life underground for his protagonist in *Invisible Man,* a protagonist who, as he types the story of his life from a hole underground, writes himself into being in the first person (in contradistinction to Richard Wright's protagonist, Bigger Thomas, whose reactive tale of fear and flight is told in the third person). Walker's novel also riffs on Ellison's claim for the revolutionary possibilities of writing the self into being, whereas Hurston's protagonist, Janie, speaks herself into being. Ellison himself signified multiply upon Richard Wright's *Native Son,* from the title to the use of the first-person bildungsroman to chart the coming to consciousness of a sensitive protagonist moving from blindness and an inability to do little more than react to his environment, to the insight gained by wresting control of his identity from social forces and strong individuals that would circumscribe and confine his life choices. Toni Morrison, master supernaturalist and perhaps the greatest black novelist of all, trumps Ellison's trope of blindness by returning over and over to the possibilities and limits of insight within worlds confined or circumscribed not by supraforces (à la Wright) but by the confines of the imagination and the ironies of individual and family history, signifying upon Faulkner, Woolf, and Márquez in the process. And Ishmael Reed, the father of black postmodernism and what we might think of as the hip-hop novel, the tradition's master parodist, signifies upon everybody and everything in the black literary tradition, from the slave narratives to the Harlem Renaissance to black nationalism and feminism.

This sort of literary signifying is what makes a literary tradition, well, a "tradition," rather than a simple list of books whose authors happen to have been born in the same country, share the same gender, or would be identified by their peers as belonging to this ethnic group or that. What makes these books special—"classic"—however, is something else. Each text has the uncanny capacity to take the seemingly mundane details of the day-to-day African American experience of its time and transmute those details and the characters' actions into something that transcends its ostensible subject's time and place, its specificity. These texts reveal the human universal through the African American particular: all true art, all classics, do this; this is what "art" is, a revelation of that which makes each of us sublimely human, rendered in the minute details of the actions and thoughts and feelings of a compelling character embedded in a time and place. But as soon as we find ourselves turning to a text for its anthropological or sociological data, we have left the realm of art; we have reduced the complexity of fiction or poetry to an essay, and this is not what imaginative literature is for. Richard Wright, at his best, did this, as did his signifying disciple Ralph Ellison; Louis Armstrong and Duke Ellington, Bessie Smith and Billie Holiday achieved this effect

in music; Jacob Lawrence and Romare Bearden achieved it in
the visual arts. And this is what Wole Soyinka does in his
tragedies, what Toni Morrison does in her novels, what Derek
Walcott does in his poetry. And while it is risky to name one's
contemporaries in a list such as this, I think that Rita Dove and
Jamaica Kincaid achieve this effect as well, as do Colson White-
head and Edwidge Danticat, in a younger generation. (There
are other writers whom I would include in this group had I the
space.) By delving ever so deeply into the particularity of the
African and African American experience, these authors man-
age, somehow, to come out the other side, making the race or
the gender of their characters almost translucent, less impor-
tant than the fact that they stand as aspects of ourselves beyond
race or gender or time or place, precisely in the same magical
way that Hamlet never remains for long stuck as a prince in a
court in Denmark.

Each classic black text reveals to us, uncannily, subtly, how
the Black Experience is inscribed, inextricably and indelibly, in
the human experience, and how the human experience takes
one of its myriad forms in blackface, as it were. Together, such
texts also demonstrate, implicitly, that African American cul-
ture is one of the world's truly great and eternal cultures, as no-
ble and as resplendent as any. And it is to publish such texts,
written by African and African American authors, that Penguin
has created this new series, which I have the pleasure of editing.

HENRY LOUIS GATES, JR.

HENRY LOUIS GATES, JR., is general editor for a series of African
American classics, including *The Portable Charles W. Ches-
nutt,* edited with an introduction by William L. Andrews, and
God's Trombones, by James Weldon Johnson, with a foreword
by Maya Angelou.

Foreword

"O BLACK and unknown bards of long ago,
   How came your lips to touch the sacred fire?
   How, in your darkness, did you come to know
   The power and beauty of the minstrel's lyre?
   Who first from midst his bonds lifted his eyes?"

The first African Americans were brought to what was to become the United States in 1619. They were taken from diverse areas on the African continent and arrived here without a common language and without shared experiences. It is miraculous that, under the broiling sun on slavery's plantations, they were able to use a strange language to write enduring poetry and compose great melodies. Today a conservative estimate of the African American presence lists the population at around fifty million.

In reading and rereading James Weldon Johnson's *God's Trombones,* I am convinced that the people survived brutish slavery and the brutality of segregation and racial injustices because they were able to write of their despair and even of their hope in their songs. They were able to preach of dismay and dreams in their sermons.

A religious person I know made an announcement that amazed and even shocked me. He said that the African Americans are the only people in the whole world and history who really practice Christianity. When I countered with the questions "What about the Catholics with their rituals and the Calvinists with their restraints, and the Bible Belt fundamentalists who believe that every word in the Bible is true and that God wrote each chapter with his own divine hands?" my correspondent said he had taken into consideration the Catholics, Calvinists, and the fundamentalists, and he still held that only the African Americans had practiced Christianity on a daily basis. None of them has done what the African Americans have done, and that is no group ever found in their hearts the gift of forgiveness.

African Americans nursed and raised a nation of strangers. Slave-owning parents trusted their defenseless young children to the care of Black women who could have neglected them, but did not, and to Black men who could have done them harm, but did not. The African Americans forgave the land that they worked, which also worked them to death. They forgave the slave owners who worked them without payment for 240 years. Their ability to forgive made many former slave owners uncomfortable because the slave behavior was incomprehensible to the slave owner. Slave owners were driven to categorize the African Americans in terms that they could understand. They were "like children," and even until today, centuries later, many descendants of the slave owners still believe that the African American is a character in nature, completely spoiled or absolutely innocent, i.e., childlike.

Meanwhile, African American poet lyricists described the anguish in their current condition by writing the mysterious *Steal Away*. "Steal away to Jesus, I ain't got long to stay here." The lyricists looked ahead at the possibility of relief and wrote,

> "I'm gonna lay down my burden,
>   down by the riverside
>   down by the riverside,
>   down the riverside.
> I'm gonna lay down my burden,
>   down by the riverside
>   down by the riverside,
>   down the riverside.
> And study war no more."

The Africans had come from monotheistic societies. There was God, and then one Great God, and while there were many lesser powers, i.e., the Goddess of the waters, the God of the forest, the God of fertility, it was understood that these were lesser powers than God itself. So, as the Catholics were known to pray to the saints, the Africans were known to ask the lesser powers to intercede for them with the Great God itself. The imagination the Africans brought from their own cultures made them ready candidates for Christianity.

The Africans, who knew that the Great God was hermaphroditical, were not challenged to believe that Jesus Christ was not the Son of God and a virgin and could not heal the sick, raise the dead and turn water into wine.

They accepted Jesus Christ as their savior, protector, Sweet Honey and the Rock, and a friend in need. Having Jesus on their side made the horror of slavery a little more bearable and even getting a little gentle revenge more possible. There is one spiritual which bears out that idea: "I'm gonna tell Jesus how you treat me when I get home. I'm gonna tell him all my troubles when I get home."

The same poets and composers who wrote the spirituals became preachers. They employed at once the musicality of the spirituals and the splendid eloquence of the spirituals. When the lyricists wrote "Swing Low, Sweet Chariot, coming for to carry me home," neither the singer nor the audience had to tax their imagination to consider death a sweet chariot or to doubt that heaven was their destination. When the minister told the biblical tales, he embellished the language with poesy so that he could say, "I looked over Jordan and what did I see, coming for to carry me home. A band of angels coming after me, coming for to carry me home . . ."

The poet composers of the spirituals could not and dared not complain about the conditions of slavery, so they wrote of the conditions in which they lived, and their prayer for relief in,

> "Go down Moses,
> way down in Egypt land,
> tell ole Pharaoh
> to let my people go.
> When Israel was in Egypt land,
> let my people go
> Oppressed so hard
> they could not stand

> let my people go
> Go down Moses
> Way down in Egypt land
> Tell ole Pharaoh,
> let my people go."

The spirit of these lyrics exists in Johnson's poem "Let My People Go." Moses was the name given to Harriet Tubman. It was also the pseudonym for any person on the Underground Railroad or person from the antislavery movement who traveled through the slave states trying to find freedom for slaves. Reading the lyrics of the spirituals and reading the poesy of the sermons is much like reading the history and chronology of slavery. The despair is never ignored, yet the majestic beams of hope illuminate the landscape.

God's Trombones is a pure time machine. With Johnson's collection of poems inspired by African American sermons and influenced by the spirituals, we are able to understand how the people survived. The lyrics to the most poignant song remains:

> "Sometimes I feel like a motherless child
> A long way from home."

The people, who wrote that pain and lived that pain, survived that unutterable loneliness.

It is hard to keep a dry eye when we think of the poet/ preachers who wrote those words, and there are few songs in the pantheon happier or more promising than:

> "I got shoes
> you got shoes,
> all of God's children
> got shoes,
> when we get to heaven,
> we're going to put on our shoes
> and dance all over God's heaven.
> I got a robe, you got a robe,
> all God's children got a robe

> When we get to heaven we're
> going to put on our robes and
> going to walk all over God's Heaven
> Heaven, Heaven, Heaven
> Everybody's talking about Heaven.
> Ain't going there
> I'm gonna walk all over God's Heaven."

I welcome this collection.

MAYA ANGELOU

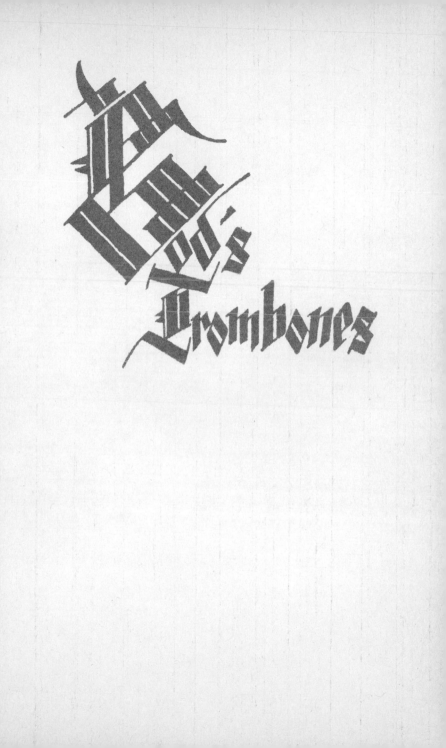

Preface

A good deal has been written on the folk creations of the American Negro: his music, sacred and secular; his plantation tales, and his dances; but that there are folk sermons, as well, is a fact that has passed unnoticed. I remember hearing in my boyhood sermons that were current, sermons that passed with only slight modifications from preacher to preacher, and from locality to locality. Such sermons were "The Valley of Dry Bones," which was based on the vision of the prophet in the 37th chapter of Ezekiel; the "Train Sermon," in which both God and the devil were pictured as running trains, one loaded with saints, that pulled up in heaven, and the other with sinners, that dumped its load in hell; the "Heavenly March," which gave in detail the journey of the faithful from earth, on up through the pearly gates to the great white throne. Then there was a stereotyped sermon, which had no definite subject and which was quite generally preached; it began with the Creation, went on to the fall of man, rambled through the trials and tribulations of the Hebrew Children, came down to the redemption by Christ, and ended with the Judgment Day and a warning and an exhortation to sinners. This was the framework of a sermon that allowed the individual preacher the widest latitude that could be desired for all his arts and powers. There was one Negro sermon that in its day was a classic, and widely known to the public. Thousands of people, white and black, flocked to the church of John Jasper in Richmond, Virginia, to hear him preach his famous sermon proving that the earth is flat and the sun does move. John Jasper's sermon was imitated and adapted by many lesser preachers.

I heard only a few months ago in Harlem an up-to-date version of the "Train Sermon." The preacher styled himself "Son of Thunder"—a sobriquet adopted by many of the old-time preachers—and phrased his subject, "The Black Diamond Express, running between here and hell, making thirteen stops and arriving in hell ahead of time."

The old-time Negro preacher has not yet been given the niche in which he properly belongs. He has been portrayed only as a semi-comic figure. He had, it is true, his comic aspects, but on the whole he was an important figure, and at bottom a vital factor. It was through him that the people of diverse languages and customs who were brought here from diverse parts of Africa and thrown into slavery were given their first sense of unity and solidarity. He was the first shepherd of this bewildered flock. His power for good or ill was very great. It was the old-time preacher who for generations was the mainspring of hope and inspiration for the Negro in America. It was also he who instilled into the Negro the narcotic doctrine epitomized in the Spiritual "You May Have All Dis World, But Give Me Jesus." This power of the old-time preacher, somewhat lessened and changed in his successors, is still a vital force; in fact, it is still the greatest single influence among the colored people of the United States. The Negro today is, perhaps, the most priest-governed group in the country.

The history of the Negro preacher reaches back to Colonial days. Before the Revolutionary War, when slavery had not yet taken on its more grim and heartless economic aspects, there were famed black preachers who preached to both whites and blacks. George Liele was preaching to whites and blacks at Augusta, Georgia, as far back as 1773, and Andrew Bryan at Savannah a few years later.* The most famous of these earliest preachers was Black Harry, who during the Revolutionary period accompanied Bishop Asbury as a drawing card and preached from the same platform with other founders of the Methodist Church. Of him, John Ledman in his *History of the Rise of Methodism in America* says, "The truth was that Harry

*See *The History of the Negro Church*, Carter G. Woodson.

was a more popular speaker than Mr. Asbury or almost anyone else in his day." In the two or three decades before the Civil War Negro preachers in the North, many of them well-educated and cultured, were courageous spokesmen against slavery and all its evils.

The effect on the Negro of the establishment of separate and independent places of worship can hardly be estimated. Some idea of how far this effect reached may be gained by a comparison between the social and religious trends of the Negroes of the Old South and of the Negroes of French Louisiana and the West Indies, where they were within and directly under the Roman Catholic Church and the Church of England. The old-time preacher brought about the establishment of these independent places of worship and thereby provided the first sphere in which race leadership might develop and function. These scattered and often clandestine groups have grown into the strongest and richest organization among colored Americans. Another thought—except for these separate places of worship there never would have been any Spirituals.

The old-time preacher was generally a man far above the average in intelligence; he was, not infrequently, a man of positive genius. The earliest of these preachers must have virtually committed many parts of the Bible to memory through hearing the scriptures read or preached from in the white churches which the slaves attended. They were the first of the slaves to learn to read, and their reading was confined to the Bible, and specifically to the more dramatic passages of the Old Testament. A text served mainly as a starting point and often had no relation to the development of the sermon. Nor would the old-time preacher balk at any text within the lids of the Bible. There is the story of one who after reading a rather cryptic passage took off his spectacles, closed the Bible with a bang and by way of preface said, "Brothers and sisters, this morning—I intend to explain the unexplainable—find out the undefinable—ponder over the imponderable—and unscrew the inscrutable."

The old-time Negro preacher of parts was above all an orator, and in good measure an actor. He knew the secret of oratory, that at bottom it is a progression of rhythmic words more than it is anything else. Indeed, I have witnessed congregations moved to ecstasy by the rhythmic intoning of sheer incoherencies. He was a master of all the modes of eloquence. He often possessed a voice that was a marvelous instrument, a voice he could modulate from a sepulchral whisper to a crashing thunder clap. His discourse was generally kept at a high pitch of fervency, but occasionally he dropped into colloquialisms and, less often, into humor. He preached a personal and anthropomorphic God, a sure-enough heaven and a red-hot hell. His imagination was bold and unfettered. He had the power to sweep his hearers before him; and so himself was often swept away. At such times his language was not prose but poetry. It was from memories of such preachers there grew the idea of this book of poems.

In a general way, these poems were suggested by the rather vague memories of sermons I heard preached in my childhood; but the immediate stimulus for setting them down came quite definitely at a comparatively recent date. I was speaking on a Sunday in Kansas City, addressing meetings in various colored churches. When I had finished my fourth talk it was after nine o'clock at night, but the committee told me there was still another meeting to address. I demurred, making the quotation about the willingness of the spirit and the weakness of the flesh, for I was dead tired. I also protested the lateness of the hour, but I was informed that for the meeting at this church we were in good time. When we reached the church an "exhorter" was just concluding a dull sermon. After his there were two other short sermons. These sermons proved to be preliminaries, mere curtain-raisers for a famed visiting preacher. At last he arose. He was a dark-brown man, handsome in his gigantic proportions. He appeared to be a bit self-conscious, perhaps impressed by the presence of the "distinguished visitor" on the platform, and started in to preach a formal sermon from a formal text. The congregation sat apathetic and dozing. He sensed that he was losing his audience and his opportunity. Suddenly he closed the Bible, stepped out from behind the pulpit and

began to preach. He started intoning the old folk-sermon that
begins with the creation of the world and ends with Judgment
Day. He was at once a changed man, free, at ease and master-
ful. The change in the congregation was instantaneous. An elec
tric current ran through the crowd. It was in a moment alive
and quivering; and all the while the preacher held it in the palm
of his hand. He was wonderful in the way he employed his con-
scious and unconscious art. He strode the pulpit up and down
in what was actually a very rhythmic dance, and he brought
into play the full gamut of his wonderful voice, a voice—what
shall I say?—not of an organ or a trumpet, but rather of a
trombone,* the instrument possessing above all others the
power to express the wide and varied range of emotions en-
compassed by the human voice—and with greater amplitude
He intoned, he moaned, he pleaded—he blared, he crashed, he
thundered. I sat fascinated; and more, I was, perhaps against
my will, deeply moved; the emotional effect upon me was irre-
sistible. Before he had finished I took a slip of paper and some-
what surreptitiously jotted down some ideas for the first poem,
"The Creation."

At first thought, Negro dialect would appear to be the pre-
cise medium for these old-time sermons; however, as the reader
will see, the poems are not written in dialect. My reason for not
using the dialect is double. First, although the dialect is the ex-
act instrument for voicing certain traditional phases of Negro
life, it is, and perhaps by that very exactness, a quite limited in-
strument. Indeed, it is an instrument with but two complete
stops, pathos and humor. This limitation is not due to any de-
fect of the dialect as dialect, but to the mould of convention in
which Negro dialect in the United States has been set, to the
fixing effects of its long association with the Negro only as a
happy-go-lucky or a forlorn figure. The Aframerican poet

*Trombone: A powerful brass instrument of the trumpet family, the only
wind instrument possessing a complete chromatic scale enharmonically true,
like the human voice or the violin, and hence very valuable in the orchestra.
—Standard Dictionary.

might in time be able to break this mould of convention and write poetry in dialect without feeling that his first line will put the reader in a frame of mind which demands that the poem be either funny or sad, but I doubt that he will make the effort to do it; he does not consider it worth the while. In fact, practically no poetry is being written in dialect by the colored poets of today. These poets have thrown aside dialect and discarded most of the material and subject matter that went into dialect poetry. The passing of dialect as a medium for Negro poetry will be an actual loss, for in it many beautiful things can be done, and done best; however, in my opinion, *traditional* Negro dialect as a form for Aframerican poets is absolutely dead. The Negro poet in the United States, for poetry which he wishes to give a distinctively racial tone and color, needs now an instrument of greater range than dialect; that is, if he is to do more than sound the small notes of sentimentality. I said something on this point in *The Book of American Negro Poetry*, and because I cannot say it better, I quote: "What the colored poet in the United States needs to do is something like what Synge did for the Irish; he needs to find a form that will express the racial spirit by symbols from within rather than by symbols from without—such as the mere mutilation of English spelling and pronunciation. He needs a form that is freer and larger than dialect, but which will still hold the racial flavor; a form expressing the imagery, the idioms, the peculiar turns of thought and the distinctive humor and pathos, too, of the Negro, but which will also be capable of voicing the deepest and highest emotions and aspirations and allow of the widest range of subjects and the widest scope of treatment." The form of "The Creation," the first poem of this group, was a first experiment by me in this direction.

The second part of my reason for not writing these poems in dialect is the weightier. The old-time Negro preachers, though they actually used dialect in their ordinary intercourse, stepped out from its narrow confines when they preached. They were all saturated with the sublime phraseology of the Hebrew prophets and steeped in the idioms of King James English, so when they preached and warmed to their work they spoke another language, a language far removed from traditional Negro dialect. It was really a fusion of Negro idioms with Bible English; and in this there may have been, after all, some kinship with the innate grandiloquence of their old African tongues. To place in the mouths of the talented old-time Negro preachers a language that is a literary imitation of Mississippi cotton-field dialect is sheer burlesque.

Gross exaggeration of the use of big words by these preachers, in fact by Negroes in general, has been commonly made; the laugh being at the exhibition of ignorance involved. What is the basis of this fondness for big words? Is the predilection due, as is supposed, to ignorance desiring to parade itself as knowledge? Not at all. The old-time Negro preacher loved the sonorous, mouth-filling, ear-filling phrase because it gratified a highly developed sense of sound and rhythm in himself and his hearers.

I claim no more for these poems than that I have written them after the manner of the primitive sermons. In the writing of them I have, naturally, felt the influence of the Spirituals. There is, of course, no way of re-creating the atmosphere—the fervor of the congregation, the amens and hallelujahs, the undertone of singing which was often a soft accompaniment to parts of the sermon; nor the personality of the preacher—his physical magnetism, his gestures and gesticulations, his changes of tempo, his pauses for effect, and, more than all, his tones of voice. These poems would better be intoned than read; especially does this apply to "Listen, Lord," "The Crucifixion," and "The Judgment Day." But the intoning practiced by the old-time preacher is a thing next to impossible to describe; it must be heard, and it is extremely difficult to imitate even when heard. The finest, and perhaps the only demonstration ever given to a New York public, was the intoning of the dream in Ridgely Torrence's *Rider of Dreams* by Opal Cooper of the Negro Players at the Madison Square Theatre in 1917. Those who were fortunate enough to hear him can never, I know, forget the thrill of it. This intoning is always a matter of crescendo and diminuendo in the intensity—a rising and falling between plain speaking and wild chanting. And often a startling effect is gained by breaking off suddenly at the highest point of intensity and dropping into the monotone of ordinary speech.

The tempos of the preacher I have endeavored to indicate by the line arrangement of the poems, and a certain sort of pause that is marked by a quick intaking and an audible expulsion of the breath I have indicated by dashes. There is a decided syncopation of speech—the crowding in of many syllables or the lengthening out of a few to fill one metrical foot, the sensing of which must be left to the reader's ear. The rhythmical stress of this syncopation is partly obtained by a marked silent fraction of a beat; frequently this silent fraction is filled in by a hand clap.

One factor in the creation of atmosphere I have included— the preliminary prayer. The prayer leader was sometimes a woman. It was the prayer leader who directly prepared the way for the sermon, set the scene, as it were. However, a most impressive concomitant of the prayer, the chorus of responses which gave it an antiphonal quality, I have not attempted to set down. These preliminary prayers were often products hardly less remarkable than the sermons.

The old-time Negro preacher is rapidly passing. I have here tried sincerely to fix something of him.

New York City, 1927.

Listen Lord
A Prayer

LISTEN, LORD—A PRAYER

O Lord, we come this morning
Knee-bowed and body-bent
Before thy throne of grace.
O Lord—this morning
Bow our hearts beneath our knees,
And our knees in some lonesome valley.
We come this morning—
Like empty pitchers to a full fountain,
With no merits of our own.
O Lord—open up a window of heaven,
And lean out far over the battlements of glory,
And listen this morning.

Lord, have mercy on proud and dying sinners—
Sinners hanging over the mouth of hell,
Who seem to love their distance well.
Lord—ride by this morning—
Mount your milk-white horse,
And ride a this morning—
And in your ride, ride by old hell,
Ride by the dingy gates of hell,
And stop poor sinners in their headlong plunge.

And now, O Lord, this man of God,
Who breaks the bread of life this morning—
Shadow him in the hollow of thy hand,
And keep him out of the gunshot of the devil.
Take him, Lord—this morning—

Wash him with hyssop inside and out,
Hang him up and drain him dry of sin.
Pin his ear to the wisdom-post,
And make his words sledge hammers of truth—
Beating on the iron heart of sin.
Lord God, this morning—
Put his eye to the telescope of eternity,
And let him look upon the paper walls of time.
Lord, turpentine his imagination,
Put perpetual motion in his arms,
Fill him full of the dynamite of thy power,
Anoint him all over with the oil of thy salvation,
And set his tongue on fire.

And now, O Lord—
When I've done drunk my last cup of sorrow—
When I've been called everything but a child of God—
When I'm done travelling up the rough side of the
    mountain—
O—Mary's Baby—
When I start down the steep and slippery steps of death—
When this old world begins to rock beneath my feet—
Lower me to my dusty grave in peace
To wait for that great gittin' up morning—Amen.

The Creation

THE CREATION

And God stepped out on space,
And he looked around and said:
I'm lonely—
I'll make me a world.

And far as the eye of God could see
Darkness covered everything,
Blacker than a hundred midnights
Down in a cypress swamp.

Then God smiled,
And the light broke,
And the darkness rolled up on one side,
And the light stood shining on the other,
And God said: That's good!

Then God reached out and took the light in his hands,
And God rolled the light around in his hands
Until he made the sun;
And he set that sun a-blazing in the heavens.
And the light that was left from making the sun
God gathered it up in a shining ball
And flung it against the darkness,
Spangling the night with the moon and stars.
Then down between
The darkness and the light
He hurled the world;
And God said: That's good!

Then God himself stepped down—
And the sun was on his right hand,
And the moon was on his left;
The stars were clustered about his head,
And the earth was under his feet.
And God walked, and where he trod
His footsteps hollowed the valleys out
And bulged the mountains up.

Then he stopped and looked and saw
That the earth was hot and barren.
So God stepped over to the edge of the world
And he spat out the seven seas—
He batted his eyes, and the lightnings flashed—
He clapped his hands, and the thunders rolled—
And the waters above the earth came down,
The cooling waters came down.

Then the green grass sprouted,
And the little red flowers blossomed,
The pine tree pointed his finger to the sky,
And the oak spread out his arms,
The lakes cuddled down in the hollows of the ground,
And the rivers ran down to the sea;
And God smiled again,
And the rainbow appeared,
And curled itself around his shoulder.

Then God raised his arm and he waved his hand
Over the sea and over the land,
And he said: Bring forth! Bring forth!
And quicker than God could drop his hand,
Fishes and fowls
And beasts and birds
Swam the rivers and the seas,
Roamed the forests and the woods,
And split the air with their wings.
And God said: That's good!

Then God walked around,
And God looked around
On all that he had made.
He looked at his sun,
And he looked at his moon,
And he looked at his little stars;
He looked on his world
With all its living things,
And God said: I'm lonely still.

Then God sat down—
On the side of a hill where he could think;
By a deep, wide river he sat down;
With his head in his hands,
God thought and thought,
Till he thought: I'll make me a man!

Up from the bed of river
God scooped the clay;
And by the bank of the river
He kneeled him down;
And there the great God Almighty
Who lit the sun and fixed it in the sky,
Who flung the stars to the most far corner of the night,
Who rounded the earth in the middle of his hand;
This Great God,
Like a mammy bending over her baby,
Kneeled down in the dust
Toiling over a lump of clay
Till he shaped it in his own image;

Then into it he blew the breath of life,
And man became a living soul.
Amen. Amen.

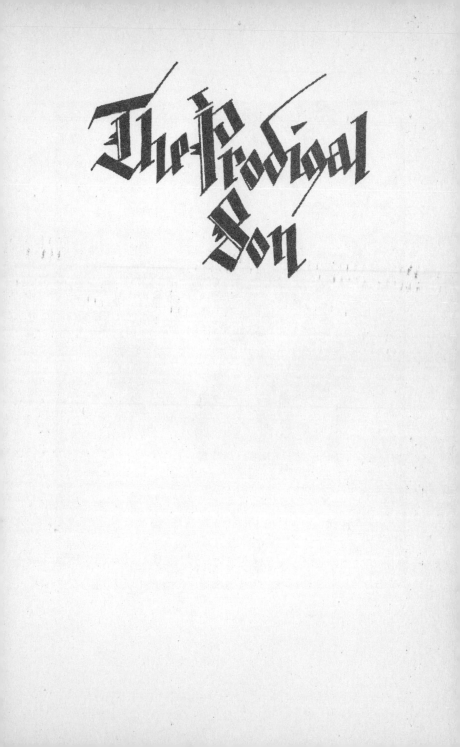

The Prodigal Son

THE PRODIGAL SON

Young man—
Young man—
Your arm's too short to box with God.

But Jesus spake in a parable, and he said:
A certain man had two sons.
Jesus didn't give this man a name,
But his name is God Almighty.
And Jesus didn't call these sons by name,
But ev'ry young man,
Ev'rywhere,
Is one of these two sons.

And the younger son said to his father,
He said: Father, divide up the property,
And give me my portion now.
And the father with tears in his eyes said: Son,
Don't leave your father's house.
But the boy was stubborn in his head,
And haughty in his heart,
And he took his share of his father's goods,
And went into a far-off country.

There comes a time,
There comes a time
When ev'ry young man looks out from his father's house,
Longing for that far-off country.

And the young man journeyed on his way,
And he said to himself as he travelled along:
This sure is an easy road,
Nothing like the rough furrows behind my father's plow.

Young man—
Young man—
Smooth and easy is the road
That leads to hell and destruction.
Down grade all the way,
The further you travel, the faster you go.
No need to trudge and sweat and toil,
Just slip and slide and slip and slide
Till you bang up against hell's iron gate.

And the younger son kept travelling along,
Till at night-time he came to a city.
And the city was bright in the night-time like day,
The streets all crowded with people,
Brass bands and string bands a-playing,
And ev'rywhere the young man turned
There was singing and laughing and dancing.
And he stopped a passer-by and he said:
Tell me what city is this?
And the passer-by laughed and said: Don't you know?
This is Babylon, Babylon,
The great city of Babylon.
Come on, my friend, and go along with me.
And the young man joined the crowd.

Young man—
Young man—
You're never lonesome in Babylon.
You can always join a crowd in Babylon.
Young man—
Young man—
You can never be alone in Babylon,
Alone with your Jesus in Babylon.

You can never find a place, a lonesome place,
A lonesome place to go down on your knees,
And talk with your God, in Babylon.
You're always in a crowd in Babylon.

And the young man went with his new-found friend,
And bought himself some brand new clothes,
And he spent his days in the drinking dens,
Swallowing the fires of hell.
And he spent his nights in the gambling dens,
Throwing dice with the devil for his soul.
And he met up with the women of Babylon.
Oh, the women of Babylon!
Dressed in yellow and purple and scarlet,
Loaded with rings and earrings and bracelets,
Their lips like a honeycomb dripping with honey,
Perfumed and sweet-smelling like a jasmine flower;
And the jasmine smell of the Babylon women
Got in his nostrils and went to his head,
And he wasted his substance in riotous living,
In the evening, in the black and dark of night,
With the sweet-sinning women of Babylon.
And they stripped him of his money,
And they stripped him of his clothes,
And they left him broke and ragged
In the streets of Babylon.

Then the young man joined another crowd—
The beggars and lepers of Babylon.
And he went to feeding swine,
And he was hungrier than the hogs;
He got down on his belly in the mire and mud
And ate the husks with the hogs.
And not a hog was too low to turn up his nose
At the man in the mire of Babylon.

Then the young man came to himself—
He came to himself and said:

In my father's house are many mansions,
Ev'ry servant in his house has bread to eat,
Ev'ry servant in his house has a place to sleep;
I will arise and go to my father.
And his father saw him afar off,
And he ran up the road to meet him.
He put clean clothes upon his back,
And a golden chain around his neck,
He made a feast and killed the fatted calf,
And invited the neighbors in.

Oh-o-oh, sinner,
When you're mingling with the crowd in Babylon—
Drinking the wine of Babylon—
Running with the women of Babylon—
You forget about God, and you laugh at Death.
Today you've got the strength of a bull in your neck
And the strength of a bear in your arms,
But some o' these days, some o' these days,
You'll have a hand-to-hand struggle with bony Death,
And Death is bound to win.

Young man, come away from Babylon,
That hell-border city of Babylon.
Leave the dancing and gambling of Babylon,
The wine and whiskey of Babylon,
The hot-mouthed women of Babylon;
Fall down on your knees,
And say in your heart:
I will arise and go to my Father.

GO DOWN DEATH—A FUNERAL SERMON

Weep not, weep not,
She is not dead;
She's resting in the bosom of Jesus.
Heart-broken husband—weep no more;
Grief-stricken son—weep no more;
Left-lonesome daughter—weep no more;
She's only just gone home.

Day before yesterday morning,
God was looking down from his great, high heaven,
Looking down on all his children,
And his eye fell on Sister Caroline,
Tossing on her bed of pain.
And God's big heart was touched with pity,
With the everlasting pity.

And God sat back on his throne,
And he commanded that tall, bright angel standing at
     his right hand:
Call me Death!
And that tall, bright angel cried in a voice
That broke like a clap of thunder:
Call Death!—Call Death!
And the echo sounded down the streets of heaven
Till it reached away back to that shadowy place,
Where Death waits with his pale, white horses.

And Death heard the summons,
And he leaped on his fastest horse,
Pale as a sheet in the moonlight.
Up the golden street Death galloped,
And the hoofs of his horse struck fire from the gold,
But they didn't make no sound.
Up Death rode to the Great White Throne,
And waited for God's command.

And God said: Go down, Death, go down,
Go down to Savannah, Georgia,
Down in Yamacraw,
And find Sister Caroline.
She's borne the burden and heat of the day,
She's labored long in my vineyard,
And she's tired—
She's weary—
Got down, Death, and bring her to me.

And Death didn't say a word,
But he loosed the reins on his pale, white horse,
And he clamped the spurs to his bloodless sides,
And out and down he rode,
Through heaven's pearly gates,
Past suns and moons and stars;
On Death rode,
And the foam from his horse was like a comet in the sky;
On Death rode,
Leaving the lightning's flash behind;
Straight on down he came.

While we were watching round her bed,
She turned her eyes and looked away,
She saw what we couldn't see;
She saw Old Death. She saw Old Death
Coming like a falling star.
But Death didn't frighten Sister Caroline;
He looked to her like a welcome friend.

And she whispered to us: I'm going home,
And she smiled and closed her eyes.

And Death took her up like a baby,
And she lay in his icy arms,
But she didn't feel no chill.
And Death began to ride again—
Up beyond the evening star,
Out beyond the morning star,
Into the glittering light of glory,
On to the Great White Throne.
And there he laid Sister Caroline
On the loving breast of Jesus.

And Jesus took his own hand and wiped away her tears,
And he smoothed the furrows from her face,
And the angels sang a little song,
And Jesus rocked her in his arms,
And kept a-saying: Take your rest,
Take your rest, take your rest.

Weep not—weep not,
She is not dead;
She's resting in the bosom of Jesus.

Noah Built the Ark

NOAH BUILT THE ARK

In the cool of the day—
God was walking—
Around in the Garden of Eden.
And except for the beasts, eating in the fields,
And except for the birds, flying through the trees,
The garden looked like it was deserted.
And God called out and said: Adam,
Adam, where art thou?
And Adam, with Eve behind his back,
Came out from where he was hiding.

And God said: Adam,
What hast thou done?
Thou hast eaten of the tree!
And Adam,
With his head hung down,
Blamed it on the woman.

For after God made the first man Adam,
He breathed a sleep upon him;
Then he took out of Adam one of his ribs,
And out of that rib made woman.
And God put the man and woman together
In the beautiful Garden of Eden,
With nothing to do the whole day long
But play all around in the garden.
And God called Adam before him,
And he said to him:

Listen now, Adam,
Of all the fruit in the garden you can eat,
Except of the tree of knowledge;
For the day thou eatest of that tree,
Thou shalt surely die.

Then pretty soon along came Satan.
Old Satan came like a snake in the grass
To try out his tricks on the woman.
I imagine I can see Old Satan now
A-sidling up to the woman.
I imagine the first word Satan said was:
Eve, you're surely good looking.
I imagine he brought her a present, too,—
And, if there was such a thing in those ancient days,
He brought her a looking-glass.

And Eve and Satan got friendly—
Then Eve got to walking on shaky ground;
Don't ever get friendly with Satan.—
And they started to talk about the garden,
And Satan said: Tell me, how do you like
The fruit on the nice, tall, blooming tree
Standing in the middle of the garden?
And Eve said:
That's the forbidden fruit,
Which if we eat we die.

And Satan laughed a devilish little laugh,
And he said to the woman: God's fooling you, Eve;
That's the sweetest fruit in the garden.
I know you can eat that forbidden fruit,
And I know that you will not die.

And Eve looked at the forbidden fruit,
And it was red and ripe and juicy.
And Eve took a taste, and she offered it to Adam,

And Adam wasn't able to refuse;
So he took a bite, and they both sat down
And ate the forbidden fruit.—
Back there, six thousand years ago,
Man first fell by woman—
Lord, and he's doing the same today.

And that's how sin got into this world.
And man, as he multiplied on the earth,
Increased in wickedness and sin.
He went on down from sin to sin,
From wickedness to wickedness,
Murder and lust and violence,
All kinds of fornications,
Till the earth was corrupt and rotten with flesh,
An abomination in God's sight.

And God was angry at the sins of men.
And God got sorry that he ever made man.
And he said: I will destroy him.
I'll bring down judgment on him with a flood.
I'll destroy ev'rything on the face of the earth,
Man, beasts and birds, and creeping things.
And he did—
Ev'rything but the fishes.

But Noah was a just and righteous man.
Noah walked and talked with God.
And, one day, God said to Noah,
He said: Noah, build thee an ark.
Build it out of gopher wood.
Build it good and strong.
Pitch it within and pitch it without.
And build it according to the measurements
That I will give to thee.
Build it for you and all your house,
And to save the seeds of life on earth;

For I'm going to send down a mighty flood
To destroy this wicked world.

And Noah commenced to work on the ark.
And he worked for about one hundred years.
And ev'ry day the crowd came round
To make fun of Old Man Noah.
And they laughed and they said: Tell us, old man,
Where do you expect to sail that boat
Up here amongst the hills?

But Noah kept on a-working.
And ev'ry once in a while Old Noah would stop,
He'd lay down his hammer and lay down his saw,
And take his staff in hand;
And with his long, white beard a-flying in the wind,
And the gospel light a-gleaming from his eye,
Old Noah would preach God's word:

Sinners, oh, sinners,
Repent, for the judgment is at hand.
Sinners, oh, sinners,
Repent, for the time is drawing nigh.
God's wrath is gathering in the sky.
God's a-going to rain down rain on rain.
God's a-going to loosen up the bottom of the deep,
And drown this wicked world.
Sinners, repent while yet there's time
For God to change his mind.

Some smart young fellow said: This old man's
Got water on the brain.
And the crowd all laughed—Lord, but didn't they laugh;
And they paid no mind to Noah,
But kept on sinning just the same.

One bright and sunny morning,
Not a cloud nowhere to be seen,

God said to Noah: Get in the ark!
And Noah and his folks all got in the ark,
And all the animals, two by two,
A he and a she marched in.
Then God said: Noah, Bar the door!
And Noah barred the door.

And a little black spot begun to spread,
Like a bottle of ink spilling over the sky;
And the thunder rolled like a rumbling drum;
And the lightning jumped from pole to pole;
And it rained down rain, rain, rain,
Great God, but didn't it rain!
For forty days and forty nights
Waters poured down and waters gushed up;
And the dry land turned to sea.
And the old ark-a she begun to ride;
The old ark-a she begun to rock;
Sinners came a-running down to the ark;
Sinners came a-swimming all round the ark;
Sinners pleaded and sinners prayed—
Sinners wept and sinners wailed—
But Noah'd done barred the door.

And the trees and the hills and the mountain tops
Slipped underneath the waters.
And the old ark sailed that lonely sea—
For twelve long months she sailed that sea,
A sea without a shore.

Then the waters begun to settle down,
And the ark touched bottom on the tallest peak
Of old Mount Ararat.
The dove brought Noah the olive leaf,
And Noah when he saw that the grass was green,
Opened up the ark, and they all climbed down,
The folks, and the animals, two by two,
Down from the mount to the valley.

And Noah wept and fell on his face
And hugged and kissed the dry ground.

And then—

God hung out his rainbow cross the sky,
And he said to Noah: That's my sign!
No more will I judge the world by flood—
Next time I'll rain down fire.

The Crucifixion

THE CRUCIFIXION

Jesus, my gentle Jesus,
Walking in the dark of the Garden—
The Garden of Gethsemane,
Saying to the three disciples:
Sorrow is in my soul—
Even unto death;
Tarry ye here a little while,
And watch with me.

Jesus, my burdened Jesus,
Praying in the dark of the Garden—
The Garden of Gethsemane.
Saying: Father,
Oh, Father,
This bitter cup,
This bitter cup,
Let it pass from me.

Jesus, my sorrowing Jesus,
The sweat like drops of blood upon his brow,
Talking with his Father,
While the three disciples slept,
Saying: Father,
Oh, Father,
Not as I will,
Not as I will,
But let thy will be done.

Oh, look at black-hearted Judas—
Sneaking through the dark of the Garden—
Leading his crucifying mob.
Oh, God!
Strike him down!
Why *don't* you strike him down,
Before he plants his traitor's kiss
Upon my Jesus' cheek?

And they take my blameless Jesus,
And they drag him to the Governor,
To the mighty Roman Governor.
Great Pilate seated in his hall,—
Great Pilate on his judgment seat,
Said: In this man I find no fault.
I find no fault in him.
And Pilate washed his hands.

But they cried out, saying:
Crucify him!—
Crucify him!—
Crucify him!—
His blood be on our heads.
And they beat my loving Jesus,
They spit on my precious Jesus;
They dressed him up in a purple robe,
They put a crown of thorns upon his head,
And they pressed it down—
Oh, they pressed it down—
And they mocked my sweet King Jesus.

Up Golgotha's rugged road
I see my Jesus go.
I see him sink beneath the load,
I see my drooping Jesus sink.
And then they laid hold on Simon,
Black Simon, yes, black Simon;

They put the cross on Simon,
And Simon bore the cross.

On Calvary, on Calvary,
They crucified my Jesus.
They nailed him to the cruel tree,
And the hammer!
The hammer!
The hammer!
Rang through Jerusalem's streets.
The hammer!
The hammer!
The hammer!
Rang through Jerusalem's streets.

Jesus, my lamb-like Jesus,
Shivering as the nails go through his hands;
Jesus, my lamb-like Jesus,
Shivering as the nails go through his feet.
Jesus, my darling Jesus,
Groaning as the Roman spear plunged in his side;
Jesus, my darling Jesus,
Groaning as the blood came spurting from his wound.
Oh, look how they done my Jesus.

Mary,
Weeping Mary,
Sees her poor little Jesus on the cross.
Mary,
Weeping Mary,
Sees her sweet, baby Jesus on the cruel cross,
Hanging between two thieves.

And Jesus, my lonesome Jesus,
Called out once more to his Father,
Saying:
My God,

My God,
Why hast thou forsaken me?
And he drooped his head and died.

And the veil of the temple was split in two,
The midday sun refused to shine,
The thunder rumbled and the lightning wrote
An unknown language in the sky.
What a day! Lord, what a day!
When my blessed Jesus died.

Oh, I tremble, yes, I tremble,
It causes me to tremble, tremble,
When I think how Jesus died;
Died on the steeps of Calvary,
How Jesus died for sinners,
Sinners like you and me.

Let My People Go

LET MY PEOPLE GO

And God called Moses from the burning bush,
He called in a still, small voice,
And he said: Moses—Moses—
And Moses listened,
And he answered and said:
Lord, here am I.

And the voice in the bush said: Moses,
Draw not nigh, take off your shoes,
For you're standing on holy ground.
And Moses stopped where he stood,
And Moses took off his shoes,
And Moses looked at the burning bush,
And he heard the voice,
But he saw no man.

Then God again spoke to Moses,
And he spoke in a voice of thunder:
I am the Lord God Almighty,
I am the God of thy fathers,
I am the God of Abraham,
Of Isaac and of Jacob.
And Moses hid his face.

And God said to Moses:
I've seen the awful suffering
Of my people down in Egypt.
I've watched their hard oppressors,

Their overseers and drivers;
The groans of my people have filled my ears
And I can't stand it no longer;
So I'm come down to deliver them
Out of the land of Egypt,
And I will bring them out of that land
Into the land of Canaan;
Therefore, Moses, go down,
Go down into Egypt,
And tell Old Pharaoh
To let my people go.

And Moses said: Lord, who am I
To make a speech before Pharaoh?
For, Lord, you know I'm slow of tongue.
But God said: I will be thy mouth and I will be thy tongue;
Therefore, Moses, go down,
Go down yonder into Egypt land,
And tell Old Pharaoh
To let my people go.

And Moses with his rod in hand
Went down and said to Pharaoh:
Thus saith the Lord God of Israel,
Let my people go.

And Pharaoh looked at Moses,
He stopped still and looked at Moses;
And he said to Moses: Who is this Lord?
I know all the gods of Egypt,
But I know no God of Israel;
So go back, Moses, and tell your God,
I will not let this people go.

Poor Old Pharaoh,
He knows all the knowledge of Egypt,
Yet never knew—
He never knew

The one and the living God.
Poor Old Pharaoh,
He's got all the power of Egypt,
And he's going to try
To test his strength
With the might of the great Jehovah,
With the might of the Lord God of Hosts,
The Lord mighty in battle.
And God, sitting high up in his heaven,
Laughed at poor Old Pharaoh.

And Pharaoh called the overseers,
And Pharaoh called the drivers,
And he said: Put heavier burdens still
On the backs of the Hebrew Children.
Then the people chode with Moses,
And they cried out: Look here, Moses,
You've been to Pharaoh, but look and see
What Pharaoh's done to us now.
And Moses was troubled in mind.

But God said: Go again, Moses,
You and your brother, Aaron,
And say once more to Pharaoh,
Thus saith the Lord God of the Hebrews,
Let my people go.
And Moses and Aaron with their rods in hand
Worked many signs and wonders.
But Pharaoh called for his magic men,
And they worked wonders, too.
So Pharaoh's heart was hardened,
And he would not,
No, he would not
Let God's people go.

And God rained down plagues on Egypt,
Plagues of frogs and lice and locusts,
Plagues of blood and boils and darkness,

And other plagues besides.
But ev'ry time God moved the plague
Old Pharaoh's heart was hardened,
And he would not,
No, he would not
Let God's people go.
And Moses was troubled in mind.

Then the Lord said: Listen, Moses,
The God of Israel will not be mocked,
Just one more witness of my power
I'll give hard-hearted Pharaoh.
This very night about midnight,
I'll pass over Egypt land,
In my righteous wrath will I pass over,
And smite their first-born dead.

And God that night passed over.
And a cry went up out of Egypt.
And Pharaoh rose in the middle of the night
And he sent in a hurry for Moses;
And he said: Go forth from among my people,
You and all the Hebrew Children;
Take your goods and take your flocks,
And get away from the land of Egypt.

And, right then, Moses led them out,
With all their goods and all their flocks;
And God went on before,
A guiding pillar of cloud by day,
And a pillar of fire by night.
And they journeyed on in the wilderness,
And came down to the Red Sea.

In the morning,
Oh, in the morning,
They missed the Hebrew Children.

Four hundred years,
Four hundred years
They'd held them down in Egypt land.
Held them under the driver's lash,
Working without money and without price.
And it might have been Pharaoh's wife that said:
Pharaoh—look what you've done.
You let those Hebrew Children go,
And who's going to serve us now?
Who's going to make our bricks and mortar?
Who's going to plant and plow our corn?
Who's going to get up in the chill of the morning?
And who's going to work in the blazing sun?
Pharaoh, tell me that!

And Pharaoh called his generals,
And the generals called the captains,
And the captains called the soldiers.
And they hitched up all the chariots,
Six hundred chosen chariots of war,
And twenty-four hundred horses.
And the chariots all were full of men,
With swords and shields
And shiny spears
And battle bows and arrows.
And Pharaoh and his army
Pursued the Hebrew Children
To the edge of the Red Sea.

Now, the Children of Israel, looking back,
Saw Pharaoh's army coming.
And the rumble of the chariots was like a thunder storm,
And the whirring of the wheels was like a rushing wind,
And the dust from the horses made a cloud that darked
    the day,
And the glittering of the spears was like lightnings in
    the night.

And the Children of Israel all lost faith,
The children of Israel all lost hope;
Deep Red Sea in front of them
And Pharaoh's host behind.
And they mumbled and grumbled among themselves:
Were there no graves in Egypt?
And they wailed aloud to Moses and said:
Slavery in Egypt was better than to come
To die here in this wilderness.

But Moses said:
Stand still! Stand still!
And see the Lord's salvation.
For the Lord God of Israel
Will not forsake his people.
The Lord will break the chariots,
The Lord will break the horsemen,
He'll break great Egypt's sword and shield,
The battle bows and arrows;
This day he'll make proud Pharaoh know
Who is the God of Israel.

And Moses lifted up his rod
Over the Red Sea;
And God with a blast of his nostrils
Blew the waters apart,
And the waves rolled back and stood up in a pile,
And left a path through the middle of the sea
Dry as the sands of the desert.
And the Children of Israel all crossed over
On to the other side.

When Pharaoh saw them crossing dry,
He dashed on in behind them—
Old Pharaoh got about half way cross,
And God unlashed the waters,
And the waves rushed back together,
And Pharaoh and all his army got lost,

And all his host got drownded.
And Moses sang and Miriam danced,
And the people shouted for joy,
And God led the Hebrew Children on
Till they reached the promised land.

Listen!—Listen!
All you sons of Pharaoh.
Who do you think can hold God's people
When the Lord God himself has said,
Let my people go?

The Judgment Day

THE JUDGMENT DAY

In that great day,
People, in that great day,
God's a-going to rain down fire.
God's a-going to sit in the middle of the air
To judge the quick and the dead.

Early one of these mornings,
God's a-going to call for Gabriel,
That tall, bright angel, Gabriel;
And God's a-going to say to him: Gabriel,
Blow your silver trumpet,
And wake the living nations.

And Gabriel's going to ask him: Lord,
How loud must I blow it?
And God's a-going to tell him: Gabriel,
Blow it calm and easy.
Then putting one foot on the mountain top,
And the other in the middle of the sea,
Gabriel's going to stand and blow his horn,
To wake the living nations.

Then God's a-going to say to him: Gabriel,
Once more blow your silver trumpet,
And wake the nations underground.

And Gabriel's going to ask him: Lord
How loud must I blow it?

And God's a-going to tell him: Gabriel,
Like seven peals of thunder.
Then the tall, bright angel, Gabriel,
Will put one foot on the battlements of heaven
And the other on the steps of hell,
And blow that silver trumpet
Till he shakes old hell's foundations.

And I feel Old Earth a-shuddering—
And I see the graves a-bursting—
And I hear a sound,
A blood-chilling sound.
What sound is that I hear?
It's the clicking together of the dry bones,
Bone to bone—the dry bones.
And I see coming out of the bursting graves,
And marching up from the valley of death,
The army of the dead.
And the living and the dead in the twinkling of an eye
Are caught up in the middle of the air,
Before God's judgment bar.

Oh-o-oh, sinner,
Where will you stand,
In that great day when God's a-going to rain down fire?
Oh, you gambling man—where will you stand?
You whore-mongering man—where will you stand?
Liars and backsliders—where will you stand,
In that great day when God's a-going to rain down fire?

And God will divide the sheep from the goats,
The one on the right, the other on the left.
And to them on the right God's a-going to say:
Enter into my kingdom.
And those who've come through great tribulations,
And washed their robes in the blood of the Lamb,
They will enter in—

Clothed in spotless white,
With starry crowns upon their heads,
And silver slippers on their feet,
And harps within their hands;—

And two by two they'll walk
Up and down the golden street,
Feasting on the milk and honey
Singing new songs of Zion,
Chattering with the angels
All around the Great White Throne.

And to them on the left God's a-going to say:
Depart from me into everlasting darkness,
Down into the bottomless pit.
And the wicked like lumps of lead will start to fall,
Headlong for seven days and nights they'll fall,
Plumb into the big, black, red-hot mouth of hell,
Belching out fire and brimstone.
And their cries like howling, yelping dogs,
Will go up with the fire and smoke from hell,
But God will stop his ears.

Too late, sinner! Too late!
Good-bye, sinner! Good-bye!
In hell, sinner! In hell!
Beyond the reach of the love of God.

And I hear a voice, crying, crying:
Time shall be no more!
Time shall be no more!
Time shall be no more!
And the sun will go out like a candle in the wind,
The moon will turn to dripping blood,
The stars will fall like cinders,
And the sea will burn like tar;
And the earth shall melt away and be dissolved,
And the sky will roll up like a scroll.

With a wave of his hand God will blot out time,
And start the wheel of eternity.

Sinner, oh, sinner,
Where will you stand
In that great day when God's a-going to rain down fire?

God's Trombones
Seven Negro Sermons in Verse
In *God's Trombones*, one of James Weldon Johnson's most celebrated works, inspirational sermons of African American preachers are reimagined as poetry, reverberating with the musicality and splendid eloquence of the spirituals. This classic collection includes "Listen Lord—A Prayer," "The Creation," "The Prodigal Son," "Go Down Death—A Funeral Sermon," "Noah Built the Ark," "The Crucifixion," "Let My People Go," and "The Judgment Day."

ISBN 978-0-14-018403-7

Available from Penguin Classics in June 2008 with a new foreword by Maya Angelou and a new General Editor essay by Henry Louis Gates, Jr.

ISBN 978-0-14-310541-1

Complete Poems
Introduction by Sondra Kathryn Wilson
This Penguin original collects all the poems from Johnson's published works—*Fifty Years and Other Poems* (1917), *God's Trombones* (1927), and *Saint Peter Relates an Incident of the Resurrection Day* (1935)—along with a number of previously unpublished poems. Sondra Kathryn Wilson, the foremost authority on Johnson and his work, provides an introduction that sheds light on Johnson's many achievements and his pioneering contributions to recording and celebrating the African American experience.

ISBN 978-0-14-118545-3

Lift Every Voice and Sing
This selection of more than forty poems includes both uncompromising indictments of racial injustice and celebrations of the triumphs of African Americans.

ISBN 978-0-14-118387-9

The Autobiography of an Ex-Colored Man
Introduction by William L. Andrews
First published in 1912, Johnson's pioneering fictional "memoir" is an unprecedented analysis of the social causes and artistic consequences of a black man's denial of his heritage.

ISBN 978-0-14-018402-0

Along This Way
The Autobiography of James Weldon Johnson
Published just four years before his death in 1938, James Weldon Johnson's autobiography is a fascinating portrait of an African American who broke the racial divide at a time when the Harlem Renaissance had not yet begun to usher in the civil rights movement. Beginning with his birth in Jacksonville, Florida, and detailing his education, his role in the Harlem Renaissance, and his later years as a professor and civil rights reformer, *Along This Way* is an inspiring classic of African American literature.

ISBN 978-0-14-310517-6

THE STORY OF PENGUIN CLASSICS

Before 1946 . . . "Classics" are mainly the domain of academics and students; readable editions for everyone else are almost unheard of. This all changes when a little-known classicist, E. V. Rieu, presents Penguin founder Allen Lane with the translation of Homer's *Odyssey* that he has been working on in his spare time.

1946 Penguin Classics debuts with *The Odyssey*, which promptly sells three million copies. Suddenly, classics are no longer for the privileged few.

1950s Rieu, now series editor, turns to professional writers for the best modern, readable translations, including Dorothy L. Sayers's *Inferno* and Robert Graves's unexpurgated *Twelve Caesars*.

1960s The Classics are given the distinctive black covers that have remained a constant throughout the life of the series. Rieu retires in 1964, hailing the Penguin Classics list as "the greatest educative force of the twentieth century."

1970s A new generation of translators swells the Penguin Classics ranks, introducing readers of English to classics of world literature from more than twenty languages. The list grows to encompass more history, philosophy, science, religion, and politics.

1980s The Penguin American Library launches with titles such as *Uncle Tom's Cabin* and joins forces with Penguin Classics to provide the most comprehensive library of world literature available from any paperback publisher.

1990s The launch of Penguin Audiobooks brings the classics to a listening audience for the first time, and in 1999 the worldwide launch of the Penguin Classics Web site extends their reach to the global online community.

The 21st Century Penguin Classics are completely redesigned for the first time in nearly twenty years. This world-famous series now consists of more than 1,300 titles, making the widest range of the best books ever written available to millions—and constantly redefining what makes a "classic."

The Odyssey continues . . .

The best books ever written

PENGUIN 🐧 CLASSICS

SINCE 1946

Find out more at www.penguinclassics.com

Visit www.vpbookclub.com

CLICK ON A CLASSIC
www.penguinclassics.com

The world's greatest literature at your fingertips

Constantly updated information on more than a thousand titles,
from Icelandic sagas to ancient Indian epics, Russian drama to
Italian romance, American greats to African masterpieces

•

The latest news on recent additions to the list, updated
editions, and specially commissioned translations

•

Original essays by leading writers

•

A wealth of background material, including biographies
of every classic author from Aristotle to Zamyatin, plot
synopses, readers' and teachers' guides, useful Web links

•

Online desk and examination copy assistance for academics

•

Trivia quizzes, competitions, giveaways, news on
forthcoming screen adaptations